chimamanda:
The Adventures of Little Mermaid's African Cousin

chimamanda:
The Adventures of Little Mermaid's African Cousin

Rudolf Ogoo Okonkwo

Winepress
by **NOIRLEDGE**

Jointly published by
Noirledge Limited, under its Winepress Publishing imprint
and Irokopost Media Group Inc., Rosedale, NY 11422

Noirledge Limited
13, Elewura Street, off Challenge Bypass, Ibadan, Nigeria
Tel: +234 809 816 4359 | +234 805 316 4359
Email: noirledge@gmail.com | www.noirledge.com

ISBN: 978-0-9768354-7-9
A catalogue record for this book is available from the National Library of
Nigeria.

Illustrations: Peipei
Cover Design: Servio Gbadamosi
Book Design: Servio Gbadamosi
Typesetting: www.noirledge.com

Dedication

To
Ijeamaka and Ogonna,
for enriching my life with so
much stories and so much joy...

Mother Knows Best: Chimamanda's mother destroying the bridge.

1

Mother Knows Best

One day, one of the most eligible bachelorettes of the River Niger Mermaid Dynasty, Chimamanda swam to the site of River Niger Bridge under construction. As she raised her head to the river surface, the bright red decorations on her head shone in the sun. She was surprised to find rubbles in the place where the uncompleted bridge once stood. She saw men who had gathered there, taking pictures and measurements. Some of the men had their hands under their chins and some had their heads bowed. They appeared to be wondering what happened to the bridge they had been building.

Chimamanda felt sorry for them. She was also unhappy because the men were everywhere due to their devastated bridge and as such she had no chance to visit the banks of the river and search for things the men had cast away which could erase the scar on her forehead.

She could not tell her mother what she saw because she was not supposed to visit the site again. But she was suspicious that her mother was the one who destroyed the bridge.

Days passed and she noticed that the men had started rebuilding the bridge. Everything was going well again. During the evening time, she visited the banks and swam along the bank searching for a cure for the scar.

This time, the men came with heavier equipment and the construction progressed faster. They also left more things by the riverbanks. Though she checked out many of those bottles of creams and drinks, none had been able to clear her scar. But she continued to search and continued to believe that men who could build something as magnificent as the bridge coming into view must have a cure for her scar.

One day she picked up a bottle by the riverbank and rubbed its content on her forehead. It started to burn. She tried to clean it with water but the heat did not go away. She swam deep inside the river and used mud from the Barrier Reef to stop the sensation. It left a wide discoloration on her forehead.

"Chimamanda, what happened to your forehead?" her mother asked.

"Nothing," she said.

"Don't lie to me young girl," her mother barked.

Chimamanda was silent.

"I bet you she had been rubbing things on that scar," Chimamanda's sister, Ada said.

"No, I haven't," Chimamanda protested.

"You've gone back to the bridge site," her mother said.

"No, I haven't," Chimamanda lied.

"We shall see," her mother said.

That night Chimamanda joined her siblings on the bed but her mind was with the humans and their bridge. She suspected that her mother would go there at night and destroy it. She pretended to be sleeping. When her mother left, she sneaked out and followed her. She was far from her mother by a great distance, careful not to cause any suspicion. She caught her mother at the site tearing down the bridge.

And Chimamanda wept.

She cried all the way as she rushed back home. She returned to her bed and slept.

In the morning, she woke up and saw her mother with a large cut on her stomach. It looked like something made by falling debris.

"Mummy, what happened to you?" Chimamanda and her siblings asked her.

"I was attacked by humans," their mother said.

"Where?" Chimamanda asked.

"At the bridge," their mother said.

"You see why you should never go there," Ifeoma said to Chimamanda.

"You're right, Ifeoma," her mother said. "If not for my strength, those wicked men would have caught me. And once I'm out of the water for seven minutes, my power would have vanished. I was just minding my business when they came from nowhere and threw their net around me and began to fire their guns."

Chimamanda shook her head in disbelief. She walked into her room and cried the more.

Hello Humans: Chimamanda meets Zik.

2

Hello Humans

C himamanda's mother spent the next few weeks nursing her wounds. During that time, Chimamanda went to the bridge site every day. She saw men walking around the site in disbelief. Again, some of the men had their hands under their chins and others had their heads bowed. They appeared to be wondering what again happened to the bridge they had been building.

Chimamanda felt sorry for them.

One day, an old man stooping around the banks saw her by the riverbanks crying.

"Why are you crying?" the old man asked.

"I'm sad because my mother tore down the bridge your people were building," Chimamanda said.

"That's alright little beauty," the old man said. "We shall rebuild it."

"But she will destroy it again," Chimamanda said in between sobs.

The old man was a medicine man named Zik. He was charged with finding a way to stop the mermaids from destroying the bridge. He was happy to have encountered the daughter of the great river goddess and he hoped to work out a plan that would stop the destruction of the bridge.

"What does your mother want?" Zik asked, resting his body on a wooden walking stick in his hand.

"She wants your people to stop building the bridge," Chimamanda said.

"Why?" he asked, his gray hair stood up on his head and all along his beard.

"Because she thinks you're going to pollute the river."

"But we just want to drive across."

"That's what I told her."

Zik thought about it for a while. The beads on his neck were of the same deep red color as Chimamanda's hair decoration. He was not sure if Chimamanda was a possible ally or if she was sent to set him up.

"What do you want in all this?" Zik asked.

"I just want your people and our people to get along."

Zik thought about it for a while. He looked deep into Chimamanda's eyes.

"If you work with me, we can bring about peace," Zik said.

"I will," Chimamanda said.

Zik told Chimamanda he would fulfill any one of her wishes if she convinced her mother to stop tearing down the bridge.

"But she will not," Chimamanda said.

"But you have not tried," Zik said.

"I've tried," Chimamanda said. "She doesn't even want me to mention it again."

Zik gave Chimamanda's words a great thought.

"What's your wish?" he asked Chimamanda.

"I want this scar on my face to go away," Chimamanda said.

"That's it?" Zik asked.

"That's it," Chimamanda said.

"Does it hurt you?"

"No."

"Does it block your view?"

"No."

"Does it slow your swimming?"

"No," Chimamanda said. "I just want it to go away."

"I will make it go away," Zik said.

"Really?"

"Yes."

"That will mean the world to me."

"Now all I want from you is to convince your mother that if she stops destroying the bridge I will erase your scar."

Chimamanda dropped her head on hearing that.

"What's the matter?" Zik asked.

"But I already told you she will not," Chimamanda said.

"But you have not told her what I will do for you in return," Zik said.

"I know my mother," Chimamanda said. "She doesn't care about my scar. She thinks it is nothing to be worried about."

Zik thought deeply about Chimamanda's words.

"I think you should give her the benefit of the doubt," Zik said.

"If you say so, though I know exactly what she would say," Chimamanda said.

"Yes," Zik said. "Tell her that you met an old man who

would erase your scar if she stops destroying our bridge. It is okay if she refuses. Just come back here in seven days and I will bring a cure for you."

Chimamanda went home a little happy and a little apprehensive about talking to her mother. She summoned the courage and told her mother.

"Chimamanda, who told you I'm the one who destroyed their bridge?" her mother scolded. "How many times will I tell you to stop going to the surface? How dare you talk to a human?"

"He was an old, fragile man," Chimamanda said.

Her mother slapped her.

"Stop talking nonsense," her mother yelled. "Why are you determined to destroy us all? What did we do to you? Haven't we cared for you? Haven't I provided you with all you need?"

Chimamanda began to cry.

"You're just one child but you're a handful," her mother continued. "Are we going to run away for you?"

Chimamanda turned around and swam off.

"Come back here," her mother yelled.

But Chimamanda did not turn around.

"If you don't come back here I will banish you from this river forever," her mother screamed.

Chimamanda ignored her and swam off.

"May fever and dysentery kill them all," Chimamanda's mother muttered.

Chimamanda's siblings, Ada and Ifeoma later found her sleeping at the Eternal corral and brought her home. She refused to eat any food for six days. Her mother pleaded with her each day. She brought her all her favorite dishes, but she still refused.

Her mother was fed up with begging her.

"She who refuses to eat denies her anus poop," her mother said.

The Python Fat Cure: Chimamanda with a python round her waist.

3

The Python Fat Cure

On the seventh day, Chimamanda went up the surface of River Niger and met Zik. The look on her face told him she had failed to convince her mother.

"I told you so," Chimamanda said.

"It's okay," Zik said. "We make sacrifices so that the blame will be that of the spirits."

Zik gave her a bottle containing python's fat. He told her to rub it on her forehead every day for six days. On the seventh day, Zik told her to come back to the riverbank.

"You will see a python waiting for you at this spot where we are. Pick the python up and let it wrap itself around you. By the time you get back home, the scar will be gone."

"That's it?" Chimamanda asked.

"With your scar gone, we hope your mother will then stop destroying our bridge."

Chimamanda thanked Zik.

"One more thing," Zik said.

"What's it?"

"Whenever the python starts hissing, you know that I

17

want to see you," Zik said.

"Ok," Chimamanda said.

"And another thing."

"Yes."

"If the python at any time lays an egg, make sure you bring it to me."

"No problem."

Chimamanda went home happy. That night, she confided with her siblings that her scar would soon disappear. In the morning, she rubbed the cream on her forehead. The next morning, her siblings woke her up with a mocking clap.

"Look," they shouted, "it is gone."

She took their taunts without complaining. Each morning she applied the cream and the next morning her siblings would mock her differently.

On the seventh day, she went back to the place where she met Zik. As he said, there was a python waiting for her by the riverbank.

Chimamanda swam close. The python crawled near her. The python told her to stretch her hand. She did. The python slithered on it.

"Don't worry," the python said. "I will wrap myself around you and rest my head on your chest. Then I will excrete fats, which you will collect in a bottle. The fat should last for seven days. Once you keep rubbing it on your forehead the scar will be gone."

Chimamanda did as the python said. She collected the fats that oozed from the python and put it inside the bottle. She wiped her fins on her forehead. She looked at the river surface to rub the fat in and found that the scar was gone.

She was ecstatic. With the python coiled around her she ran back into the river to show her mother.

"Look at me," Chimamanda screamed. "Look at me now."

Her mother and sisters looked at her and saw the python around her body.

"Yuck!" they gasped.

"Go and return that thing where you got it," her mother ordered.

"That's disgusting," Ada said.

"It must be an abomination to tie that creepy thing around you," Ifeoma said.

"It healed my scar," Chimamanda shouted. "I'm healed, I'm healed. Can't you all see it?"

Ada and Ifeoma looked at her forehead.

But her mother did not. In fact, she became furious.

"I don't care what it did for you," her mother yelled, "just return it where you found it."

"But mom...," Chimamanda cried.

"I don't want to hear any but. Just do what I said," her mother ordered.

"But I need to keep the python to collect the healing substance," Chimamanda pleaded. "It comes from its body."

"That thing is not staying in this house," her mother said.

"And I need you to stop destroying the bridge, too."

"Oh Oh, it came from those men you've been talking to?" her mother said. "So, you have continued to defy me."

"But mummy, the old man was right," Chimamanda said. "Are you happy that I'm healed?"

"You're healed from what?" her mother asked. "I never

knew anything was wrong with you."

"My scar, mama," Chimamanda said. "My scar."

"I would rather die in my delusion than to believe that these humans mean any good," her mother said.

"Please!" Chimamanda pleaded.

Her mother spat.

"Before this spittle gets to the surface, let it be that you have disappeared from here and returned that thing wherever you got it," she said.

Chimamanda swam away, sobbing.

That night, her mother went to the bridge site and leveled all that the men had built. She dragged some of their equipment into the river. It was the worst devastation she had ever caused.

Looking at it, it was clear she wanted to end their attempt at building the bridge forever.

The next morning, the python began to hiss incessantly. Chimamanda knew what it meant. She had to meet with Zik.

Plan B: Chimamanda and the python.

4

Plan B

At the riverbank Chimamanda saw Zik. His face was in a frown, exposing very pronounced wrinkles. His lips were pursed and his eyes were heavy.

"You haven't held up your end of the bargain," Zik said.

"I need more time," Chimamanda said.

"It's too late."

"What do you mean it is too late?" Chimamanda asked.

"Look around," Zik said.

Chimamanda looked around and saw that the beams that went into the river had been pulled down. The Rigs and heavy equipment on the bank were no more.

"Where did everything go?" Chimamanda asked.

"Your mother dragged them into the river," Zik said.

Chimamanda broke down in tears.

"My people are furious," Zik said. "They think I am not doing what I promised them."

"I'm so sorry," Chimamanda cried.

"I'm sorry, too," Zik said.

"I'll do anything to make it right," Chimamanda said.

"If you ask me, I think it is late for you and me."

"It's never late."

"My people have lost confidence in my ability to make your mother stop."

"I'll come up with something," Chimamanda said.

"If your scar that disappeared did not pacify her, I don't know what will," Zik said.

"Please give me a day to come up with something," Chimamanda pleaded.

"I don't have a day myself."

"What do you mean?"

"My contract has been cancelled."

"What does that mean?"

"I want my python," Zik said.

"Python?"

"Yes, the python," Zik said

"Which python?" Chimamanda asked in confusion.

"The one around your waist," Zik said.

"No. No. You cannot."

The python began to untangle itself around her.

"It's over," Zik said.

He stretched his hand and the python climbed up his hands as it untangled away from Chimamanda.

"What will happen to me?"

"Why should I care?"

"Will my scar reappear?" Chimamanda asked.

"It has already reappeared," Zik said.

Chimamanda looked at her reflection on the river surface and saw the scar. She screamed in horror. Her voice reverberated down the river.

"Please don't take my python away," Chimamanda pleaded.

"Take me instead. Take me, too."

"Why should I take you?" Zik said. "I don't need you for anything."

Chimamanda paused. A thought came into her.

"What if you take me and pretend that I am your hostage. When my mother comes to rescue me, you will make her pledge not to destroy your bridge anymore," Chimamanda said.

Zik gave the idea a thought.

"It sounded like a good idea but my people have lost confidence in what I'm doing. I don't think they will opt for it."

"Actually, that is a good idea," said a voice by the shrub near the banks. Chimamanda was rattled. And so was Zik. They looked at the direction where the voice came from and saw two white men.

Chimamanda dashed into the river. Zik called out to her.

"Don't run," Zik said. "I know them. They are the ones who hired me."

Chimamanda heard him but did not turn around. She continued to swim down. It did not make sense to Chimamanda that those white men whose great-grandfathers sat down in Berlin, Germany to divide Africa up for themselves in what was called "The Scramble for Africa," without consulting the Africans were now in Africa working together.

At the same time the echoes of Chimamanda's early scream for help was just getting to her mother at the grooves of the Delta where the river joined the sea.

"My little mermaid is in trouble," her mother said

where she was. "I must go and save her."

At the bank of the river, Zik scolded the two white men.

"You scared her away," Zik said. "She was about to voluntarily give herself up to get her mother to come and negotiate with us."

"We only wanted to help," one of the men said. "We thought you were about to blow a big chance."

"I know how to do these things," Zik said.

"You're too gentle and too trusting with those beings," one of the men said.

"That's how it is done," Zik said.

"No, it is not," the other man said. "Mungo Park would not have discovered this river if he had wasted his time in theatrics like this."

"When your enemies are many, you buy some bouquet."

"No, when your enemies are these vicious, you don't show them a smiling face but a face you have when you poop," one of the men said, quoting an African proverb.

"I agree," the other said. "When someone bites you in the head without caring about the hair, then you bite him in the bottom without caring about poop," the other man said.

"You all have spent too much time in Africa," Zik joked.

"I think we should not wait for her to give herself up. I think we should kidnap her right away," one of the men said.

"So how do we get her back?" the other man asked.

"She will be back," Zik said.

5

Our Common History

Long ago, there was only one daddy and mummy squirrel, one lizard and rat, a family of dinosaurs and one forest in the whole world. All the mermaids of the world lived under the sea off the coast of Madagascar. This was when Madagascar was still attached to southern Africa and before the deep plates, called plate tectonics, that Great-Grandpa mermaid built, started to move inside the bedrock of the earth.

Then, the earth was one large lump of land surrounded by water and the mermaids were one happy family. In their home, under the sea, they could hear the footsteps of dinosaurs above the earth. The sound of dinosaurs pounding the land as they did their morning exercise used to be the alarm clock that woke the mermaids up. As the earth's bedrock continued to split and drift away in what is called continental drift, different families of mermaids drifted away with the landmasses that were later called continents. The distance caused the mermaids of Africa to be disconnected from the mermaids of America, descendants of Ariel, for the first time.

Over time, millions of years to be specific, the

mermaids started to see humans. They noticed that humans began to emerge as the dominating creature on earth long after the dinosaurs had become extinct. When humans from Europe started to come to Africa by ship to look for spices and gold, the mermaids off the coast of Madagascar had concerns. They could not agree on whether the European explorers were a good thing or a bad thing. Those who disagreed used their tails to overturn some of the ships of these early explorers.

Many of these explorers were interested in buying goods. They eventually set up trading posts, went back to Europe and told wonderful adventurous stories of what they saw in Africa. But soon, the stories began to describe the people they met in Africa in a negative way, criticizing their lifestyle, beliefs and cultures. The mermaids did not like the primitive pictures of Africa that they painted in their stories. The mermaids thought that they did not care to spend quality time in Africa to understand the continent and its people. Still, the mermaids could not agree on what to do.

Meanwhile, the mermaids of the Americas lured Italian explorer, Christopher Columbus, away from his search for a sea route to India into the "New World." It was just a bet by two mermaids playing with their powers to control a boat with the twitching of their eyelids. This began a terrible shift in the interactions between Europeans and Africans. The "New World," motivated the explorers to want to settle and create their own nation outside of Europe. Driven by greed and prejudice, they began to kidnap African men and women to go to the "New World" and force them to work on sugar, coffee, tobacco, cocoa and cotton plantations.

When the mermaids of Madagascar learned of Europeans treating Africans inhumanely, they were furious. They saw Africans cry out for help, they saw them try to fight back to prevent from being kidnapped, they saw families being torn apart with those who could not get away being kidnapped and put inside rickety ships for a journey to Europe and the "New World" of the Americas.

Finally, the mermaids off the coast of Madagascar were unified to act. Their reporters across the Atlantic sea sent them stories of kidnapped and enslaved African who died and were dumped into the sea. They filed reports of kidnapped Africans who decided to jump off the boat into the sea than continue to embark on the journey with all the torture and suffering involved. The mermaids began to design weapons to stop slave traders from engaging in the kidnapping and enslavement of other humans.

According to legends, one of the weapons African mermaids used were the waves that travelled along the Atlantic sea. The mermaids would flap their fins in anger causing a hurricane. The arrival of the first hurricane was the first time the mermaids in America, the great grandparents of the little mermaid Ariel, knew that their cousins were still living in their original hometown in Africa.

Since the discovery, the two groups of mermaids began communicating via their fiber optic internet network called the mermanet. However, the hurricanes did not stop even after the Transatlantic Slave Trade ended. Every year, the mermaids in Africa would flap their fins and cause massive hurricanes in America. They were still upset at the millions of their people that died at sea during 400 years of slavery. Prophets in the mermaid world predicted that the solution to the hurricanes lied in establishing a relationship between the mermaids and humans who now ran the world.

All that changed with the birth of Chimamanda, a direct descendant of the Great Grandpa mermaid. Chimamanda is of the 20th generation with little mermaid, Ariel.

Disaster at Ikuputa Nwa: Chimamanda's dad raises her up for naming purposes.

6

Disaster at Ikuputa Nwa

Chimamanda was born at the peak of the era when European explorers were visiting Africa. One of those explorers was called Mungo Park. Mungo Park was a Scottish explorer who came to Africa in search of the legendary West African city that was built of gold, Timbuktu. On November 19, 1803, he embarked on his second exploration to Niger River. He was determined this time, to trace the path of Niger River from its origins in the Gulf of Guinea to its end in the Delta area of the Atlantic Ocean.

It was that era, when the newly born mermaid of River Niger dynasty turned two-week-old. In honor of this, her mother, father, brother and two sisters took her to the part of the river near Bussa in the heart of the Yaour Kingdom for a naming ceremony called *ikuputa nwa*.

They formed a circle at the center of the river where the tides were low. The moon glimmered over the river making the frogs croak which added rhythm to the night. The family ate sushi served by their servants and sang mermaid songs known all along the banks of the Niger. They danced the mermaid dance, flapping their tails and wriggling their waists.

The family of the mermaids of River Benue, Gambia River, and their relations from River Nile were at the ceremony. They presented ornaments, cowries and mirrors to the new-born. However, worried about boat traffic on the river, the three mermaid families were careful to stay further away from the surface of the river below the point where the canoes and peddles of local fishermen would reach.

At the height of their celebration, the mermaid's father threw the baby mermaid up in the air as tradition required. She ascended six feet above the water surface high enough for the slave coffle in the Mungo Park's boat to see her. But he was too drunk on native beer to differentiate the mermaid from a hippopotamus. The coffle called the attention of Mungo Park to what he saw. But Mungo Park was busy looking at his compass. When he finally looked up, a snake-like lightning crawled through the night sky. A roaring thunder followed soon, drowning the words of the coffle.

The newly born mermaid fell back into her father's hands. He held her up and named her Chimamanda. Her name stood for, "my destiny won't disappear." It was her father's hope that through her, the mermaids' destiny would not go extinct.

The circle of mermaids, some friends and some relatives clapped and whistled and chanted. Their shrill voices travelled like seismic waves across the length of the river. They were so loud that they did not hear the swift arrival of Mungo Park's H. M. Schooner Joliba boat. The forty-foot long, six feet wide boat slammed into the

Disaster at Ikuputa Nwa: Chimamanda in the hands of her mum.

gathering killing Chimamanda's father and brother. The impact left a wide gush on Chimamanda's forehead.

When Mungo Park's boat killed the beloved patriarch of River Niger dynasty, the mermaid who brought them wealth, health and fertility, the people of Bussa were so angry that they raised an army and waited for him at Bussa Rapids. As Mungo Park and his crew got there, the Bussa people's army opened fire. Mungo Park and his crew returned fire. Loud firework filled the air, rattling all the animals in the forest around the river. When Mungo Park and his crew ran out of ammunition, he jumped into the river and drowned.

Chimamanda's mother shrilled in horror at the sight of her husband floating on the river. Her cry pierced the night sky like a sword passed through a pillow. The other mermaids quickly swept in to carry baby Chimamanda and her mother away from further danger.

The death of Chimamanda's father was a big loss to the mermaid family. Before his death, he was working on bringing the mermaids and humans together. He believed that billions of years from now, that the continents, still drifting, would come together again as one. He wanted to make everyone know that and treat the environment well in preparation for another coming together of all creations. Some of the elders at his funeral expressed the wish that his last daughter, Chimamanda, would carry on with his work.

After the funeral, Chimamanda's mother, the goddess of River Niger moved the remainder of her family to the lower Niger, near the city of Onitsha in present-day Nigeria.

The Dilemma of a Mother: Chimamanda's mother with her kids in the river.

1

The Dilemma of a Mother

Many years after the accident, Chimamanda and her two sisters, Ada and Ifeoma, lived with their mother in River Niger. It was a large and deep river that flowed from the Gulf of Guinea in the northern part of West Africa. It formed a conference at Lokoja with River Benue. It then flowed down to the Atlantic Ocean through the mangrove swamps of the Delta.

All over the world, every river had its own mermaids. Chimamanda's mother was the mermaid of River Niger. Some called her the Mami Wota, the water goddess. Some called her the Queen. She ruled over all the creatures in Niger River. Because her husband was dead, every day, she traveled the length of the river making sure that all was well in her kingdom which kept her very busy.

Though it had been 150 years since the boat incident, Chimamanda's mother still distrusted humans. She noted that a new band of men had arrived with bigger boats. These men she was sure did not know any song of the mermaids. She detested the noise they made and their constant intrusion into her space. She believed that these

36

men did not realize that mermaids shed tears and when they were washed ashore they came up as foams.

She worked hard to prepare her daughters for life as rulers of their own seas, rivers, or streams. Life in the water had changed a lot since the days of her youth. The new men that arrived have bigger and better fishing tools. They also had firearms. They built dams across the river that disturbed the flow of water. Because of these men she could no longer sit on the rock and groom herself.

She was worried that her children were not going to survive if they did not learn to be strong, wise, courageous and vigilant.

The water goddess would have to choose between Ada, Ifeoma, and Chimamanda who would inherit River Niger when she died. The other two not picked would find another river or a stream to rule.

The three sisters were competing for the chance to inherit River Niger from their mother. The Queen would decide based on who among them could keep the mermaid tradition going. She would also consider who was courageous and who had the wisdom to exert control of the river. The final criteria the Queen would use to determine who she would name her successor would be which of them was social enough to attract a husband with whom she would continue the lineage.

8

The Scar

Chimamanda was confident about her ability to meet all the criteria to become the Queen of River Niger. Well, all the criteria, except for the part of attracting a husband. She was beautiful, some said she was more beautiful than her two sisters except for the scar on her forehead. Her insecurities regarding her scar grew as she grew.

As a younger mermaid, she once scrubbed it with a sponge until her forehead bled.

"What're you doing to yourself?" her mother yelled when she saw her bleeding face.

"I want to get this thing off," Chimamanda cried.

"Chi-Chi, I've told you it's just a scar," her mother said. "You cannot get it off."

Her mother called her the short form of her name, Chi-Chi when she wanted to be tender.

"It makes my face look ugly," Chimamanda said.

"No, it doesn't," her mother said to her.

"Yes, it does."

"It makes you distinguished."

"I don't want to be distinguished," Chimamanda cried

out. "I want to be like you, spotless."

"Everyone has a spot," her mother said. "Nobody is created perfect."

"But Ada is perfect, Ifeoma is perfect and you're perfect," she cried. "It is only me that is not perfect."

"How could you say such a silly thing, my daughter?"

"But it is true," Chimamanda said. "Ok, what is not perfect about you?"

"I have small waist," her mother said.

"But that is not visible," Chimamanda said. "It is not going to stop a potential husband from marrying anyone."

"My daughter, any trifle can stop anyone from marrying you," her mother said. "That is why they are called potential husbands. The only one that matters is the real husband who actually marries you.

"And what's not perfect in Ada?"

"Her fins are not long," her mother said.

"But husbands don't care about fins."

"Yes, they do," her mother said. "You're just not old enough to know."

"What about Ifeoma?" Chimamanda asked. "She has long fins."

"But her hair does not grow long."

"I want this scar to go away," Chimamanda cried. "Let me have short fins. Let my hair be short. But I do not want this scar."

"Look, Chimamanda," her mother stated in a matter of fact tone, "I have more important things to do with my time."

Her mother's lack of interest to help made Chimamanda go in search of answers in the mermaid library. She read every book she could see with the hope of finding an answer. At a point she blamed her inability to see the solution on the man called Julius Caesar. In Chimamanda's view, he was the stupid man who burnt down the library at Alexandra when he set his ship on fire to frustrate Achilles. Chimamanda did not care that it was an accident because Julius Caesar did not intend to burn the library. All that Chimamanda knew was that if those books were still around, one of them would have contained the cure for her scar.

9

Mission Alert

As Chimamanda grew older, her obsession with the scar intensified. She believed she would eventually find something that would erase the scar. Her conviction got a boost during the end of year party in the middle of the Atlantic Ocean. During the party, her cousin from River Nile told her that humans had something that could make the scar disappear.

From then on, she began to visit the surface of the river in hope to find what her cousin spoke of during the party.

Her mother warned her that it was dangerous to do so especially with the increase in the number of ships that sailed through the river. Chimamanda ignored her and continued to sneak out to the surface. She was careful not to let any human see her. When she saw that men had left the banks, she would go close and examine the things the men left by the riverside to see if anyone could be used to erase her scar.

One day, she saw a bottle of balm. She picked it up and was playing with it when a man appeared from nowhere. She was rattled. She jumped back into the river just as the man bolted.

After that incident, Chimamanda noticed that more men were at the bank of the river most of the time. She wondered what was bringing them there. Her curiosity ended when she saw that the men were building a bridge over the river. That day, she swam home and told her mother.

"A bridge?" her mother asked.

"What do they need a bridge for?" Ada asked.

"To drive over the river," Chimamanda said.

"How do you know?" Ifeoma asked.

"Because I know such things," Chimamanda replied.

"They want to pollute our waters," their mother said.

There was a flash of anguish over her face. She gnashed her teeth, bit her fins and shook her head.

That night, Chimamanda's mother went to the construction site and knocked down the bridge.

In the morning, she called a meeting. She thanked Chimamanda for being vigilant and for bringing the bridge construction to her attention.

"I don't want you all to ever go near that site," she warned.

"Why?" Chimamanda asked.

"Because it is a dangerous place."

"What makes it dangerous?" Chimamanda asked.

"You ask too many questions," Ada said.

"Yes," Ifeoma said. "Just do what Mummy said."

"She who asks questions never gets lost," Chimamanda said.

"To live, I have to think. To think, I have to question. To question, I have to doubt. To doubt, I have to observe. By observing, I discover. By discovering, I live."

"Here she goes again, Mungo Park's daughter," Ifeoma said.

"Stop calling me that name," Chimamanda said.

"Mungo Park's daughter," Ada said.

"Mummy, tell them to stop calling me that name," Chimamanda pleaded.

"You two stop calling her that," their mother cautioned Ada and Ifeoma.

"But you told us Mungo Park caused the injury that left the scar on her," Ada said.

"Just cut it off, you two," their mother said.

Ada and Ifeoma began to sulk. Their mother noticed.

"What humans are doing is dangerous because first they will build a bridge and soon they will want to take over the river," the Queen said looking sternly at Chimamanda. "And we must not let them take over the river. Not as long as I'm alive. And I hope you all will not let it happen even when I am no longer here."

"We won't," Ada and Ifeoma said together. Their mother heard her daughters, but she had not seen any sign that they had interest in exploring and protecting their territory. The two were just interested in collecting objects of sacrifices that people left by the riverside at night, granting people their wishes and grooming themselves. The real work of guarding the river had not been their strong point.

"But what if they only want to pass from one side to the other?" Chimamanda asked.

"You never listen to Mummy," Ada said. "She just told you that they would pollute our water."

"With what, though?" Ifeoma asked.

"With smoke from their cars' exhaust pipes and banana peels they will throw across the bridge and into the river," Ada said.

"Oh," Ifeoma said.

"But bridges expand frontiers," Chimamanda said. "Those who build bridges are heroes."

"Heroes are those who search for new and precious things to cherish and respect," their mother said. "But the men out there are vagabonds in search of fame. They go about destroying the things they do not understand. They knock down fences without first finding out why they were up."

"It's not like they are building bridges everywhere," Chimamanda said.

"I'm done talking about this," their mother said. "Just stay away from there or you will be in trouble."

Chimamanda spent one week without going there. During that time, she read more books. In one of the books she read, she discovered that in 1517, Bartolome de Las Casas, a Spanish colonist ordained as a priest in Haiti witnessed the devastation European arrival was causing to the Indian population in the "New World" through the introduction of new diseases and sheer brutality. He petitioned Charles V, the King of Spain. He asked Charles to spare the Indians by providing an alternative – Black slaves from Africa.

Charles V granted license to the Asientos to import 4000 Africans to the West Indian colonies. The first cargo arrived in 1518. For another 360 years, cargoes after cargoes arrived into the "New World". It was estimated that a total of 15 to 20 million Africans were kidnapped and enslaved over 400 years of slave trade. For the first time, Chimamanda understood how Reverend Father Bartolommeo se las Casa's concern for the fate of Indians led to Slave trade.

During the week, her mother had been secretly monitored Chimamanda and believed that her daughter got the message about how dangerous these men were and would never go to the riverside.

The Old Man and the Goddess: Chimamanda in the tank.
Her mother beside her.

10

The Old Man and the Goddess

Deep in the river where Chimamanda ran to when those two white men appeared beside Zik, She remembered her scar. She found her reflection and glanced at it. She got horrified the more. Then she heard the echo of her mother's voice.

"My little mermaid, do not worry," her mother screamed. "I'm coming to rescue you."

"Don't worry?" Chimamanda muttered to herself. "When did you begin to care about me? And how do you rescue someone who is inside your prison."

Just like Zik said that she would be back, she turned around and swam towards the banks of the river. Along the way, she thought of one of the world-famous African who was enslaved that she read about, Olaudah Equiano. She believed that he belonged to Zik's people. During slave trade, because they had no army or central government, invaders faced little resistance when they came into Igboland to kidnap Africans to take to Haiti, Brazil and America. Just like Equiano did, she hoped to write her own story about what she went through over her scar. She would call it, "The Interesting Narrative of the Life of

Chimamanda, or Chi-Chi, the African Little Mermaid."

"Take me and keep me," Chimamanda said, as she busted to the surface of the river, in front of Zik and the two white men.

Zik and the two white men were startled. They quickly recovered and carried Chimamanda off the shore and into a see-through water tank. As they lifted her off she told them that her mother was on the way to rescue her. Once inside the tank, they did not wait long before a great splash hit the banks of the river. It was the goddess.

"Where is my daughter?" the water goddess asked.

Zik pointed at the water tank.

"Get those men away from her," she ordered.

"Why?"

"They are Mungo Park's people."

"You presume."

"I don't presume," she said. "I know."

"No, they are German engineers," Zik said.

"Free my daughter now," she ordered.

"Then what was the purpose of capturing her and putting her in a tank?" Zik asked.

She saw that the old man was not intimidated.

"What do you want?" she asked.

"Now you're talking," Zik said.

"What do you want? She yelled. "I don't have all day."

"I want you to stop destroying our bridge," Zik said.

"It's over my river and I didn't give you the right to build over it."

"Your river divides our land and we didn't give you the right to divide it."

"Why am I even arguing with you?"

"I guess we should take your pretty girl into town and keep her in our museum," Zik said.

The old man turned around and signaled the two men beside the tank to start pulling it into town.

"Wait," Chimamanda's mother said. "What do you want from me?"

"I want a pledge not to tear down our bridge again."

She thought about it. She looked at the tank and saw tears swollen around Chimamanda's eyes.

"Okay," she said.

"Okay, what?" Zik asked.

"Okay, I will not tear down your bridge anymore," she said.

"What should happen if you do that again?" Zik asked.

"What else do you want? My word is my bond," Chimamanda's mother yelled.

"But?"

"But what?" she screamed. "It's not every day that I come out talking to you quarrelsome humans. I've told you that my word is my bond. Take it or leave it."

Zik walked over to the two men for consultation. One of them seemed not to agree. Chimamanda's mother could see it from the gestures of his hand and the expressions on his face. Zik and the other man finally convinced him.

Zik walked to Chimamanda's mother.

"We shall free her," Zik said.

"About time," Chimamanda's mother said.

"But if you destroy our bridge again, we won't be this kind."

Chimamanda's mother looked away.

"Did you hear what I said?" Zik asked.

"Just get me my daughter and let me go," she said.

Zik signaled at the two men. They dragged the tank toward the river.

"A stubborn fish mellows inside the fisherman's net," Zik said.

Chimamanda's mother said nothing. She watched with boiling anger as the two men opened the tank and poured the content right into the river. Chimamanda hit the water and smiled. She raised her head to the surface.

"Thank you all," she said.

Her mother did not let her finish expressing her gratitude. She grabbed her by the ears and dragged her off.

"You let them humiliate me," her mother said.

11

Grounded

At home, Chimamanda was placed in detention. Sharks that her mother hired watched her around the clock. All day and night, she was sad. But she never gave up hope of ever seeing Zik and her python. She knew that her present condition was not going to be the end of her story. She was not going to be in detention forever.

Now that she knew that her scar could be healed, she was sure that a way to achieve that would open.

In the meantime, she spent time at the reef, reading the diaries her father left behind. In one of the diaries, she saw that her father was about to disprove the fallacy that it was the angry flapping of mermaid fins that caused hurricanes on the Atlantic and Typhoons on the Pacific. Chimamanda was surprised to find out that her father was a budding scientist and a lot more.

"I may not be able to get the earth back to being one single piece of land surrounded by water," her father wrote in one diary entry, "But with ease of movement, I hope I can contribute to helping us all, men and mermaids, live in harmony as if it is still a single piece of land surrounded by water." Chimamanda gave the words of her father a great thought. She liked some of the works her father was doing but would rather be a social scientist than a pure scientist. Her interest was in studying creatures and their habitats.

Days later, the rattling of heavy machines told Chimamanda's mother that men had returned to construct the bridge. She gave them three days. Builders poured concrete columns and beams. On the fourth day, she went to the site and dug holes inside newly poured concretes. Newly poured cement leaked into the river. Once again, the whole structure collapsed.

For the men, they decided not to rebuild the bridge until they come up with a final solution to the mermaid problem.

Seven weeks passed and nothing opened up for Chimamanda. Her detention was reduced to daytime detention. She did not try to escape. She believed that when the time was right something would happen.

Over time, her mother's anger dissipated. Her mother was happy that the men had abandoned the plan to build the bridge. She began to address Chimamanda again as Chi-Chi and started to smile again at her jokes. And there were again talks about who among the daughters would inherit the river when their mother passed. A merman from River Benue named Nosa had started to visit them. He was a handsome merman from a noble family. He was checking out his potential bride. It reminded Chimamanda of her scar. Seeing the merman play with Ada told her it was because of her scar that he was leaning towards her older sister.

One day, while the family was getting ready to sleep,

Chimamanda heard the python's hiss. She immediately knew what it was. She pretended to be sleeping. When she felt her sisters were deeply asleep she sneaked out to meet the python.

"What are you doing here?" she asked the python.

"Zik sent me," the python said.

"What does he want?"

"She wants to thank you for your cooperation," the python said. "The bridge is completed and an opening ceremony is planned next month."

"I'm happy it ended well for your people," Chimamanda said.

"What do you mean?" the python asked.

"It didn't end well for me," Chimamanda said.

"I thought it ended well for everybody."

"My scar is still here."

"Oh, that's a minor thing."

"Minor?"

"Yes. Listen first," the python said, "The builders want to build your statue at the entrance of the bridge. They want you to come and pose for an artist who will mold your statue. Our description of your beauty did not come out well in what he did."

"My statue?"

"Yes," the python said. "It is their way of honoring you."

Chimamanda thought she heard a movement. It sounded as if someone stretched. She listened to know if she would hear more.

"I did not do anything to deserve it," she said.

"Oh, you did," the python said. "If you had not deceived your mother into thinking you were kidnapped, do you think she would have been pacified?"

"Shhhhhhhhhh," Chimamanda said.

There was a movement. Chimamanda signaled the python to leave. As she turned around, she saw her mother.

"So that was it? So, you were part of the plan?" she yelled. "You evil child. Thank goodness I did not keep my word with those deceptive men."

She swung at Chimamanda and failed. Chimamanda dodged and swam away.

Plan C: Chimamanda's mother in a bottle.

12

Plan C

Chimamanda swam toward the bridge. Her mother followed. Because Chimamanda was swifter, she got the bank of the river long before her mother. She saw the python waiting. She looked up and there was no bridge.

"Where's the bridge?" she asked the python.

"It's coming."

"What do you mean when you say it is coming?"

"We built it somewhere else," the python said. "We will bring the parts here and put them all together."

Also, at the bank were Zik and the artist. The artist had a drawing paper in hand. Chimamanda swam toward them.

"Ready to pose?" Zik asked.

"No," Chimamanda said, panting. "My mother is mad. She overheard the python saying that I deceived her by pretending I was kidnapped to get her to stop tearing down the bridge. She is coming up here."

"But she did not stop," Zik said. "She continued to destroy the bridge. But our people said that when the hunter learns to shoot without aiming, the bird learns to fly without perching."

"What are we going to do now?" Chimamanda asked. "She will kill me if she lays her hands on me."

"Don't worry," Zik said, "we have a plan."

Once again, they carried Chimamanda off the riverbanks and put her inside the tank. The artist walked over to the tank and began to sketch. In no time, Chimamanda's mother busted out in the open.

"Say goodbye to your daughter," Zik said.

"Who told you I care about her?" she said. "Let her carry her Mungo Park's drifters' mark and go away from me. If I had laid my fins on her she would have been in bigger trouble."

"She has become ours," Zik said.

"Please take her," she said. "I don't ever want to see her again."

"You know, some call you the Queen of the river, the goddess, but you are not that powerful," Zik said.

"Oh yeah, I'm not?" she asked, "So why is your bridge not standing here?"

Zik and Chimamanda's mother argued and traded insults. Zik insisted that they would build the bridge there. Chimamanda's mother was defiant and irritated.

Zik threw a challenge to her that would determine who was more powerful—man or mermaid. He took a bottle of Coke from his goatskin bag. He placed it on the sand and said he would squeeze himself into the bottle and then come out. He told Chimamanda's mother if she could do the same, man would give up trying to build a bridge over the river.

Chimamanda's mother agreed to the challenge. She watched as the old man squeezed himself into the bottle. Then, he climbed out. Without a pause, Chimamanda's mother squeezed herself inside the bottle. But before she could climb out, Zik covered the top of the bottle.

Once secured in the bottle, Chimamanda was released from the tank. Zik assured her that they would free her mother as soon as the bridge was installed. Work began on the installation immediately.

Back in the river, Chimamanda fought with her sisters. They blamed her for betraying their mother.

"Look," Chimamanda said to her sisters, "If these men could forgive those who went to a faraway place like Berlin to have a meeting where they shared their continent during the scramble for Africa, we should probably learn something from them."

"They are foolish men," Ifeoma said. "That is all there is to learn from them."

"The scramble for Africa was a crazy phenomenon," Chimamanda said. "Continental drift divided us but theirs was a deliberate decision by their fellow humans who went on to colonize them. Yet, they got over it. But we haven't gotten over our little area displacement from our other cousins."

"Shut up your ignorant mouth," Ada said.

"They will free her when the bridge is completed," Chimamanda said. "We have to be strategic these days. We can lead a rebellion against men, like Nat Turner, the African slave did in Virginia. But we cannot afford to lose the few of us left. The choice is ours."

But her sisters did not listen. They accused her of

reading too many books and messing up her head. They teamed up and chased her to the lower part of the river.

Chimamanda's mother was kept in the bottle until the bridge was assembled and installed. One day after it was tested, she was released.

On getting home, the first thing she did was to banish Chimamanda from the river. She declared Chimamanda wanted, dead or alive.

The Transformation: Chimamanda is human with legs.

13

The Transformation

Chimamanda went back to Zik. She told him that she had been kicked out of the river.

Zik was sorry for her.

"But I don't own a river to give you," Zik said.

"I delivered the bridge for you," Chimamanda said. "What did I get in return? Nothing. My scar was not healed. Now, I am homeless."

"What do you want me to do for you?" Zik asked.

"Just yesterday, I would have asked that you heal my scar," Chimamanda said. "But today, that has become a minor thing. I need a home first."

"But I said I do not own a river."

"Then make me a human."

"Who told you I have such powers?"

"I saw you get in and out of that little bottle, so I believe you can do it."

Zik explained to her what being a human would entail. She would not be the young maiden mermaid but a woman of equivalent age in human years. She would have to learn to fend for herself as a human.

Chimamanda agreed to everything. "It's not like I have a better option," she said.

Zik asked her to turn around and face the river. She did. He brought out a python's egg from his goatskin bag and cracked it. He poured the yoke in a calabash and added palm oil. He mixed them and poured the content on her hair. Chimamanda turned into a middle-aged woman with long legs. Her light skin reflected the rays of the sun. She gazed intensely with her deep brown eyes.

Chimamanda grabbed a mirror in her bag and looked at herself.

"I look like them," She grumbled.

"Like who?"

"Like those white people."

"What's wrong with that?"

"I don't want to be Mungo Park's daughter."

"Who do you want to be like?"

"I want to be like you."

"Like me?"

"Yeah," Chimamanda said. "Like one of your daughters."

"But I have only sons."

"I want to look the way your daughter would have looked like if you had one."

Zik grabbed dust from the ground and splashed it on her. Her skin tone changed from light skinned to charcoal-dark hue.

Chimamanda looked in the mirror and screamed so loud that the waves on the surface of River Niger reversed course.

"What's wrong?" Zik asked.

"When I said black, I don't mean black like that," Chimamanda said.

"Well, those are the two options in my trick bag," Zik said.

"Then let me remain the way I was," Chimamanda pleaded.

Zik grabbed another handful of dust, splashed it on her and her skin color returned to the original light skinned hue. Chimamanda exhaled.

Zik took a necklace off his pocket and hung it on her neck.

"Whatever you do, don't ever take this necklace off," Zik warned her.

She nodded.

"And do not ever break a python's egg," Zik said.

"Why?" She asked.

"If I tell you why, I will defy the whole charm."

"But how do I see you if I need to? Chimamanda asked.

"You cannot. My job here is done," Zik said. "But as long as you have that necklace, a little part of me will stay with you."

"But what if I need you?"

Zik searched through his bag. He found a mirror and handed it to her.

"I'm going on a very long journey," Zik said. "When I get there, I will appear to you through this mirror."

She thanked Zik.

Gradually, Chimamanda learnt to walk. She made her way down from the bridge and headed into Onitsha town. The bustling city baffled her. There were rows and rows of houses. Cars ply the roads, some crossing the bridge over River Niger to the other part of town. She was surprised that she fitted in. She even saw people who looked like her. The more she observed people, the more she adopted their mannerism. When she passed by people called her Mungo Park's daughter.

At Nkpor junction, she turned right and made her way through the towns of Nkpor and Ojoto. She was excited about what she saw. She spent time looking at humans roaming about. She watched cars pass by. She dragged her feet on the ground. When it was hot, she picked up a pair of slippers near the trash and wore them. She walked for a long time until she became tired. When hungry, she begged for food. Sometimes she got some. Other times villagers rebuked her and called her a mermaid. She told herself that she was an undercover mermaid.

After seven weeks, she began to miss her mother and sisters. She wanted to go back to the river and see them. But she knew she was far away from the Niger and she did not know how to change back into a mermaid.

At Uke town, tropical rain fell on her for two days. She spent the next day gathering bamboo, twigs, and grasses. She wanted to build a hut near a primary school, but a kind woman offered her a space in her home. At the house, the woman fed her and spread a mat on the floor for her. She slept so well. She dreamt about the river and her family. She also dreamt that Nosa kissed her. In the morning, villagers besieged the woman's house and accused her of housing a witch. Some said she was a mermaid. The woman got scared that the villagers might lynch Chimamanda.

The woman let Chimamanda go.

Back on the road, a group of boys snatched her bag. They opened it in search of money. They saw that the only valuable in it were two mirrors—her own and the one Zik gave her. The boys took Zik's mirror out. When they looked into the mirror, they saw a python hissing. They quickly dropped the bag and the mirror and fled. Chimamanda picked up her belongings.

At night, on the sky underneath which she slept, the stars came together in the shape of a mermaid. And after each rainfall, a rainbow always formed on the sky with its curve enclosing where Chimamanda was. These were signs only strong medicine men could see.

She continued to walk. The air was becoming dense. The vegetation had changed into thick palm trees, cashew trees and shrubs that goats and sheep feast on. She could feel water moving beneath the earth. Toads were croaking. Frogs were leaping from one cocoyam leaf to another. She headed down to Ideani town towards the water.

It was in the 1960s when African nations were gaining their independence from European colonial powers. Africans were questioning everything the Europeans created on their continent. It was hard for many Africans to swallow the rationale in declaring that a white man discovered a river that had existed for centuries before the first European saw it. While some Africans were renaming ancient African lakes and mountains that Europeans named after themselves, others ridiculed anyone who had European physical features as a child of Mungo Park.

That was how small children at Ideani began to call Chimamanda Mungo Park's daughter. She needed to take her bath for children had begun to call her a crazy daughter of Mungo Park. Nobody gave her food. When she went into a farm to get some corn they kicked her out. Some men even captured her and tried to chain her hands. She broke loose and fled. She was surprised at her strength.

At the border of Nnobi and Uke, she beheld Mgbo stream. It was not the mighty River Niger that she was used to. But she was happy to see moving water. She took her shower. She dipped her feet in the stream for a long time. She remembered her mother and sisters. She wished her feet and hands would turn into fins again and she would swim up the stream until she got to a river that would lead her to her family. She spent hours crying. She pondered about her obligation to her family. She missed their solidarity. She remembered the stories she had heard about her father. She felt her quest to erase her scar was a frivolous pursuit.

People came to the stream, fetched water and went back home. She wished she too could go back home.

Desperation Sets in: Chimamanda has Ify in a bottle.

14

Desperation Sets in

One day three little girls, Ify, Nkem and Chioma came to the stream to fetch water. They arrived carrying their clay pots on their heads. They spent time swimming and going after little fish. They also built sand houses by the stream. Ify caught two little fish and put them in an empty bottle she was carrying inside her clay pot. She wanted to take them home, feed them and watch them grow.

The sunset happened so quickly that the girls hurried off for home. Half way up the hill, Ify remembered her bottle of fish that she left by the bush. She decided to return to the stream and get the bottle. Her friends asked her to forget about it, but she objected. She pleaded with them to accompany her but they refused.

"That crazy daughter of Mungo Park by the stream is dangerous at dawn," Nkem warned Ify.

"How do you know?" Ify asked.

"Because my grandmother said that at night crazy people turn into spirits," Nkem said.

"I would have gone with you," Chioma said, "but I have to pound yam for my mother. I'm already late."

Ify decided to go back all alone. Along the way she sang to keep her courage up:

> *Akwaeke olima*
> *Akwaeke olima*
> *Nde olimama nde olima*
>
> *Ọ kwa gị ka nne gị na-akpọ... nde olima*
> *Nde olimama nde olima*
>
> *Ọ kwa gị ka nna gị na-akpọ... nde olima*
> *Nde olimama nde olima*
>
> *Python's egg oh*
> *Python's egg oh*
> *My precious one, oh precious one*
> *Aren't you the one that your mother calls*
> *My precious one, oh precious one*
> *Python's egg oh*
> *Python's egg oh*
> *My precious one, oh precious one*
> *Aren't you the one that your father calls*
> *My precious one, oh precious one.*

Chimamanda was lying on cashew leaves inside the forest. She was dreaming of life in the river with her family. She wished she could jump into the river and find a route from it to where her family was. She remembered the story of Igbo Landing, about those Igbo slaves on the shore of Dunbar Creek on Georgia's St. Simons Island in 1803 who turned around and walked back into the sea after seeing the life that awaited them as slaves. She wished she could do what they did right now —just jump into the stream and return home.

In her dreamlike state, she heard Ify's singing. She woke up. She listened to the song very carefully. The girl was calling on python's egg. Chimamanda believed that through her she may be able to meet the python and see if he could help her get back to Zik and to the river.

Chimamanda sat up and waited for Ify to come down.

As soon as Ify arrived and picked up her bottle, Chimamanda approached her.

"Hello little girl," Chimamanda called.

Ify panicked.

"Don't be afraid," Chimamanda said. "I just have a question for you."

Ify did not say anything. She stood on the same spot, frozen.

"Do you know where the python is?" Chimamanda asked.

Her question frightened Chimamanda.

"No ooo," she said. "Leave me alone. I do not know anything."

"But you were calling python's egg," Chimamanda said.

"It was just a song," Ify pleaded.

Ify turned around and began to run. Her tiny legs were hitting the ground fast.

Chimamanda got up and pursued her. She noticed that she was using minimal effort but covering a great distance.

Ify looked back and saw that Chimamanda was behind her. She dropped the bottle and screamed.

Chimamanda stretched her hands and grabbed her.

"I will not hurt you," Chimamanda said.

"Leave me alone," Ify cried.

"Where's the python?" Chimamanda asked.

"I don't know."

"I want you to take me to the python."

"I don't know any python."

"If you take me there I will let you go home."

"I said I do not know where the python is," Ify cried. "It is just a song."

Chimamanda held her hand. Ify fell on the ground as if her bones were taken out of her body. Chimamanda picked her up. She was so light in Chimamanda's hand. Chimamanda wondered where she got the power.

"You're going to take me to the python," Chimamanda said.

Ify continued to cry.

Chimamanda heard what appeared to be a footstep coming down the hill. She also heard a man whistling. She panicked.

She picked up the bottle that Ify had dropped. She opened it, walked to the banks of the stream and poured the content back to the stream.

Ify intensified her crying.

The footsteps were getting closer.

"Stop crying," Chimamanda said.

Ify ignored her.

Chimamanda panicked. She was afraid of being seen with the crying little girl. Her concern was that villagers could accuse her of attempting to kidnap the girl. In her fear, she felt a powerful wave enveloping her. It felt as if she was in the presence of her mother. She received a barrage of commands. After resisting initially, she relented and followed the commands.

She picked Ify up and stuffed her inside the bottle. She closed it and put it in her handbag:

Akwaeke olima

Akwaeke olima

Nde olimama nde olima

Ọ kwa gị ka nne gị na-akpọ... nde olima

Nde olimama nde olima

Ọ kwa gị ka nna gị na-akpọ... nde olima

Nde olimama nde olima

Python's egg oh

Python's egg oh

My precious one, oh precious one

Aren't you the one that your mother calls?

My precious one, oh precious one

Python's egg oh

Python's egg oh

My precious one, oh precious one

Aren't you the one that your father calls?

My precious one, oh precious one.

At Ify's village of Ngo, her family waited for her to return from the stream but did not see her. They asked her friends, Nkem and Chioma. The two girls told of how she decided to walk back to the stream to pick up her bottle of little fish. Ify's brother, Obi and her father went to the stream to look for her.

They searched everywhere but did not see her.

The next day, Obi and his friends continued the search. They went through all the forests around the village. At the village of Umuagu, they saw Chimamanda sleeping by the roadside. They asked her if she had seen a little girl going down the stream.

"Who?" Chimamanda asked. "Python's egg?"

Obi and his friends were sure something was wrong with her. When they set out to leave, they heard someone who sounded like Ify singing Python's Egg song.

"Did you hear that?" Obi asked his friends. "That sounded like Ify."

They turned back and returned to Chimamanda. But the song had stopped. They asked her again if she had seen a little girl, about ten years old, wearing a green dress.

"Who?" Chimamanda asked again. "Python's egg?"

Once again, Obi and his friends set out to leave. Again, they heard the song.

"That woman is weird," one of Obi's friends said.

"I think she is crazy," another of Obi's friend said. "She is the one people call Mungo Park's daughter."

"She is either messing with our minds or she knows what happened to Ify," Obi said.

They finally ignored her and moved on.

Return to the River: Chimamanda sleeping, native doctor confronts her.

15

Return to the River

Days after, a rumor reached all the villages of Nnobi that Mungo Park's daughter could make a little girl sing the Python's Egg song by simply hitting her handbag. All that the villagers needed to do was to give her food, pomade, powder, a local perfume, and an ankle bracelet.

Chimamanda travelled from village to village getting fed and collecting ankle bracelets from villagers who were marveled by her magic. She also began to dance when the girl sang. She stamped her feet on the ground and the ankle bracelets jingled.

"She dances like a fish," villagers said.

When she got to Ify's village of Ndam, people assembled at the village square to watch her perform. She struck her bag, and just as was rumored, a girl began to sing the python's Egg song.

Chimamanda began to dance, wriggling her waist and chest like a rope in the wind.

"She dances like a fish," one villager said.

"She dances like a mermaid," another villager said.

"Have you ever seen a mermaid?" the first villager asked.

"No," the second villager said.

"Then how do you know that she dances like a mermaid?" the first villager asked.

Meanwhile, Obi and others who had heard the singing had told Ify's parents that the girl who was singing was their daughter. They had approached a famous medicine man in their village for help.

Following the medicine man's instructions, Ify's parents had prepared fufu, egusi soup and palm wine and brought the meal to the event. After the performance, Chimamanda sat down and ate to her heart's desire. She received golden anklets from the old medicine man. Then, she fell asleep.

The medicine man carefully went into Chimamanda's bag and took out the coke bottle. He placed it on the ground, circled it with goose feathers and began to chant.

Villagers who knew the power of the medicine man gathered. When nobody was watching, Obi went where Chimamanda was sleeping and removed her necklace and put it in his pocket.

Done with his chants, the medicine man put his hand inside his goatskin bag and took out an egg. He broke it and poured the contents in a calabash. He added a few drops of palm oil into the calabash and mixed the two. He sprinkled the mixture on the bottle. He took another egg, broke it and sprinkled the contents on the ground, calling on his ancestors. He took a third egg, broke it and sprinkled the contents on Chimamanda. As soon as the egg's yoke touched Chimamanda, she woke up.

She opened her eyes, let out a strange scream that forced everyone to plug their fingers into their ears. She began to wangle on the ground like a worm. Her eyes rolled as she roared and growled. In no time her legs and hands changed into fins. She spun around wildly. Then, she fell into an ecstatic trance.

At the spot where her bottle was, now stood Ify in her green dress with her clay pot on her head. Everyone was shocked and dumbfounded. Ify's parents embraced her as they all watched Chimamanda completely turned into a mermaid. Villagers wanted to descend on the mermaid and kill it, but the medicine man stopped them.

"Don't lay your hands on the mermaid," he said. "She was trapped in a human body and was only searching for a way home."

He asked a truck driver to go and get his truck for them so that they could take the mermaid back into the stream.

As villagers waited in awe for the truck to come, they heard a scream in the crowd. It was Obi who was screaming. A python was crawling out of his pocket. It was the same pocket where he had put in Chimamanda's necklace.

The python touched the ground and crawled very rapidly to the mermaid. It wrapped itself round her and she held its head and tail in her two hands.

Villagers loaded the mermaid in the truck, poured water on her and drove her down to Mgbo stream. There they tipped the truck and let her roll into the stream.

Waiting at Mgbo stream were her mother, her two siblings and Nosa. They had heard her cry and quickly found their way to the water nearest to her.

Chimamanda in a truck heading back to the river.

They all embraced Chimamanda and welcomed her back. They told her that Nosa had been traveling to every river and every stream searching for her. He had said he would not marry anyone but Chimamanda.

Nosa and Chimamanda got married and moved to River Benue. There, they lived happily ever after.

Epilogue: The fountain.

16

Epilogue

The people of Nnobi told each other this story of a mermaid who became Mungo Park's daughter, and then, a mermaid again. They told it from one generation to the next. The town union later raised funds and built a mermaid park at the town square with the statue of the mermaid in the middle. The artist had the mermaid resting on a huge rock with a mirror in her hand and a comb near her hair. Around her tail was a water fountain. One of the spots where water was gushing out of was the mouth of the rubber python that entangled her waist.

The women of Ndam village travelled all the way to Asaba town at the bank of River Niger and learned the mermaid dance from those villagers who lived around the river. The dance dramatized Asaba people's own stories of their encounters with the mermaid.

The women of Ndam have been performing that dance till this day.

The End

About the Author

Rudolf Ogoo Okonkwo teaches Post-Colonial African History and Contemporary African Diaspora Literature at the School of Visual Art in New York City. He is the author of *This American Life Sef!* and *Children of a Retired God*. He hosts the Dr. Damages Show on  SaharaTV and writes a weekly column, *Correct Me If I'm Right* for Saharareporters.com. He lives in New York City.

Made in the USA
Middletown, DE
27 November 2021